The European Union

Political, Social, and Economic Cooperation

The
EUROPEAN UNION

POLITICAL, SOCIAL, AND ECONOMIC COOPERATION

Austria

Belgium

Cyprus

Czech Republic

Denmark

Estonia

The European Union: Facts and Figures

Finland

France

Germany

Greece

Hungary

Ireland

Italy

Latvia

Lithuania

Luxembourg

Malta

The Netherlands

Poland

Portugal

Slovakia

Slovenia

Spain

Sweden

United Kingdom

LATVIA

by
Heather Docalavich

Mason Crest Publishers
Philadelphia

Mason Crest Publishers Inc.
370 Reed Road, Broomall, Pennsylvania 19008
(866) MCP-BOOK (toll free)
www.masoncrest.com

First printing
1 2 3 4 5 6 7 8 9 10

Library of Congress Cataloging-in-Publication Data

Docalavich, Heather.
   Latvia / by Heather Docalavich.
       p. cm.—(The European Union: political, social, and economic cooperation)
   Includes bibliographical references and index.
       ISBN 1-4222-0053-1
       ISBN 1-4222-0038-8 (series)
1. Latvia—Juvenile literature. 2. European Union—Latvia—Juvenile literature. I. Title. II. European Union (Series) (Philadelphia, Pa.)
   DK504.56.D63 2006
   947.96—dc22
                                        2005016856

Produced by Harding House Publishing Service, Inc.
www.hardinghousepages.com
Interior design by Benjamin Stewart.
Cover design by MK Bassett-Harvey.
Printed in the Hashemite Kingdom of Jordan.

CONTENTS

Introduction 8

1. The Landscape 11

2. Latvia's History and Government 19

3. The Economy 31

4. Latvia's People and Culture 39

5. The Cities 47

6. The Formation of the European Union 55

7. Latvia in the European Union 69

A Calendar of Latvian Festivals 74

Recipes 76

Project and Report Ideas 79

Chronology 81

Further Reading/Internet Resources 82

For More Information 83

Glossary 84

Index 86

Picture Credits 87

Biographies 88

LATVIA

European Union Member since 2004

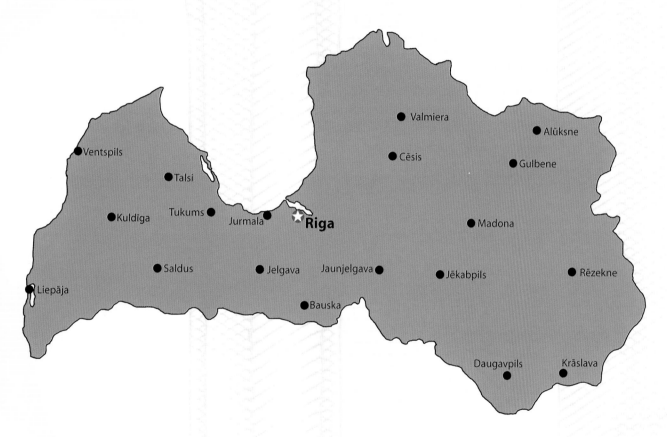

Ventspils

Talsi

Kuldīga

Tukums

Jurmala

Saldus

Liepāja

Jelgava

Bauska

Jaunjelgava

Valmiera

Cēsis

Alūksne

Gulbene

Madona

★ Riga

Jēkabpils

Rēzekne

Daugavpils

Krāslava

INTRODUCTION

Sixty years ago, Europe lay scarred from the battles of the Second World War. During the next several years, a plan began to take shape that would unite the countries of the European continent so that future wars would be inconceivable. On May 9, 1950, French Foreign Minister Robert Schuman issued a declaration calling on France, Germany, and other European countries to pool together their coal and steel production as "the first concrete foundation of a European federation." "Europe Day" is celebrated each year on May 9 to commemorate the beginning of the European Union (EU).

The EU consists of twenty-five countries, spanning the continent from Ireland in the west to the border of Russia in the east. Eight of the ten most recently admitted EU member states are former communist regimes that were behind the Iron Curtain for most of the latter half of the twentieth century.

Any European country with a democratic government, a functioning market economy, respect for fundamental rights, and a government capable of implementing EU laws and policies may apply for membership. Bulgaria and Romania are set to join the EU in 2007. Croatia and Turkey have also embarked on the road to EU membership.

While the EU began as an idea to ensure peace in Europe through interconnected economies, it has evolved into so much more today:

- Citizens can travel freely throughout most of the EU without carrying a passport and without stopping for border checks.

- EU citizens can live, work, study, and retire in another EU country if they wish.

- The euro, the single currency accepted throughout twelve of the EU countries (with more to come), is one of the EU's most tangible achievements, facilitating commerce and making possible a single financial market that benefits both individuals and businesses.

- The EU ensures cooperation in the fight against cross-border crime and terrorism.

- The EU is spearheading world efforts to preserve the environment.

- As the world's largest trading bloc, the EU uses its influence to promote fair rules for world trade, ensuring that globalization also benefits the poorest countries.

- The EU is already the world's largest donor of humanitarian aid and development assistance, providing 55 percent of global official development assistance to developing countries in 2004.

The EU is neither a nation intended to replace existing nations, nor an international organization. The EU is unique—its member countries have established common institutions to which they delegate some of their sovereignty so that decisions on matters of joint interest can be made democratically at the European level.

Europe is a continent with many different traditions and languages, but with shared values such as democracy, freedom, and social justice, cherished values well known to North Americans. Indeed, the EU motto is "United in Diversity."

Enjoy your reading. Take advantage of this chance to learn more about Europe and the EU!

Ambassador John Bruton,
Head of Delegation of the European Commission, Washington, D.C.

The Baltic Sea dominates the landscape of western Latvia. The beach at Jurmala, a resort area near the capital of Riga, is favored by many Latvians in the summer. Even the country's president has a residence in Jurmala.

THE LANDSCAPE

Welcome to Latvia. The "middle child" of the three Baltic States, both in location and size, Latvia is essentially a bridge—a place that connects east to west, ancient to modern. The beauty of the Latvian countryside can best be appreciated for its subtleties, rather than for dramatic changes of scenery.

Slightly larger than the state of West Virginia, with a population numbering less than three million, Latvia is not a large country. Most of the nation is sparsely populated, and as a result, large undeveloped areas of land remain. These undeveloped areas give us a glimpse into Europe's past. Many habitats have been preserved in Latvia that have died out in other areas of Europe due to intensive farming practices and the expansion of urban centers.

SEASHORES, PLAINS, AND FORESTS

The geographic features seen in Latvia today are the result of glacial activity that occurred in Latvia's prehistoric past. The low-lying beaches and tidal marshes of the coastal region gradually transform into a fertile, rolling plain. As much as 75 percent of Latvia's total territory is comprised of this plain; its gently rolling hills were formed as ancient glaciers pushed up mounds of soil and debris.

The resulting landscape is a vibrant green patchwork of farmland, forests, and meadows. Wildflowers are abundant, wreaths and bouquets are commonly available for sale in most village markets. Birch groves separate individual farms, and the silvery trees are commonly tapped for their juice, a favorite national beverage. Nearly three thousand lakes dot the landscape, and a number of large rivers cross the countryside, keeping the soil so moist that drainage can be a pressing problem.

In addition to birch groves, many **coniferous** forests are found in Latvia. The pine and spruce species found here not only provide valuable wood for export but also are a major source of energy; in many areas, wood is still used extensively as the primary source of heat. These evergreen forests are also unique for the types of plant species found in their **understory**. Unlike the pine forests of North America, where many different shrubs and green plants line the forest floor, Latvian forests are characterized by a lack of underbrush. Instead, the forest floor is teeming with less obvious forms of life such as lichens, mushrooms, and moss, providing a unique habitat for many unusual birds, lizards, snails, and insects.

Ten percent of the countryside is made up of mires, peat bogs, and swamps. These areas are largely untouched by human civilization, and as a result, they preserve many exotic species of wildlife that cannot be found elsewhere.

RIVERS AND LAKES

Latvia boasts thousands of lakes and a wide network of interconnected rivers and waterways.

The Vasnu Bridge crosses the mighty Daugava River, which flows through Riga. The largest city in the Baltics, Riga for centuries has been one of the primary ports on the Baltic Sea.

Over the centuries, great cities have developed along these water routes. Today, they provide transportation and opportunities for recreation, serving as indicators of the region's overall environmental health.

The most important river is the Daugava. A busy transport waterway, it has been a critical trade route for several thousand years. Originating in Russia, the river travels through Belarus before entering Latvia, where it flows directly through Riga, the nation's capital, before emptying into the Baltic Sea at the Gulf of Riga. The Daugava is also an important source of hydroelectric power. Other important Latvian rivers are

Latvia's climate is cool and the winters are long,
but much produce is raised in home gardens like this one near Dauvgapils in eastern Latvia.

the Lielupe, the Venta, the Gauja, and the Aivieskte. Since all of these rivers enter Latvia from a neighboring country, the need for international cooperation to manage the water supply and control pollution is critical. The significance of such cooperation was brought home to Latvians in 1990, when a factory in Belarus accidentally spilled more than one hundred tons of cyanide derivatives into the Daugava. The Belarus government did not warn environmental officials in Latvia, and only the massive numbers of dead fish and river animals alerted the public to the potential hazard.

QUICK FACTS: THE GEOGRAPHY OF LATVIA

Location: Eastern Europe, bordering the Baltic Sea, between Estonia and Lithuania
Area: slightly larger than West Virginia
  total: 24,938 square miles (64,589 sq. km.)
  land: 24,552 square miles (63,589 sq. km.)
  water: 386 square miles (1,000 sq. km.)
Borders: Belarus 88 miles (141 km.); Estonia 211 miles (339 km.); Lithuania 281 miles (453 km.); Russia 135 miles (217 km.)
Climate: maritime; wet, moderate winters
Terrain: low plain
Elevation extremes:
  lowest point: Baltic Sea—0 feet (0 meters)
  highest point: Gaizinkalns—1,024 feet (312 meters)
Natural hazards: none

Source: www.cia.gov, 2005.

A COOL CLIMATE

Latvia has a cool climate with a long, dark winter season. Because of its **proximity** to the sea, Latvia receives abundant precipitation. In fact, an average of 180 days each year receive precipitation, an additional forty-four days a year are foggy, and only seventy-two days a year are completely sunny. During the long winter season, from November to late April, the temperature rarely climbs above 39°F (4°C), and darkness falls around 3:30 P.M. The sun will not rise again until approximately 9:00 A.M., leaving few day-light hours in between. The summer days are longer, and daytime highs average between 57° and 71F° (14°–22°C) during these months, although the warm weather is punctuated by persistent showers.

TREES, PLANTS, AND WILDLIFE

More than 40 percent of Latvia is covered with woodlands. The composition of these forests varies, and native trees include species of pine, spruce, birch, ash, linden, oak, and yew. The entire region is carpeted with wildflowers, and

The Latgale uplands of Latvia are known for their placid lakes and deep forests.

berries and mushrooms grow in abundance. Many exotic plant species also thrive here, including more than thirty species of orchids, the rare grape-fern, the European water chestnut, and the great horsetail.

Latvia's wildlife is equally impressive. The river pearl, a large species of freshwater mussel, was once a profitable export commodity, and Latvia provided many of its coveted pearls to the royal courts of Sweden and Russia. Today the species is highly endangered; only five pearl beds survive in the entire country. The Eurasian beaver, however, once hunted almost to extinction for its pelt and distinctive flavor (it was considered a delicacy by the noble classes), has been successfully reintroduced and is now thriving. The adder is a poisonous snake found in Latvia, and herring, cod, flounder, and ocean perch inhabit the coastal waters.

The country is also home to a number of rare animals, some of them endangered species. Examples of Latvian wildlife include the European red deer, the European roe deer, the fire bellied toad, the running toad, the European wolf, the black stork, the white stork, the corncrake, and the lynx. To better protect these important national treasures, Latvia currently maintains forty-three nature parks, hundreds of smaller nature reserves, and three national parks.

Latvia's now peaceful landscape was the scene of many historical invasions. It was frequently pressured by powerful neighbors such as Russia and Germany.

2 LATVIA'S HISTORY AND GOVERNMENT

Latvia has not always existed as the country it is today. For centuries, the area was subject to invasion by larger, more powerful nations, which defined the destiny of Latvia and its people. Having emerged in 1990 as a newly independent state for only the second time in its long history, Latvia is now a united, democratic country, a member of the United Nations, and a new member of the European Union (EU). As a nation, Latvia is committed to peace and building good relations with other countries.

ANCIENT LATVIA

Human habitation of Latvian lands began around 9000 BCE, as prehistoric hunters moved into the area following the withdrawal of the glaciers. The Baltic tribes first arrived around 2000 BCE, and these forefathers of modern Latvians were the first recorded people of the territory. Around this time, the area became a famous trade crossroads; the Daugava River was known as the "route from the Vikings to the Greeks" and is mentioned in ancient chronicles as stretching from Scandinavia across modern-day Latvia through Russia to Greece.

By 900 CE, the ancient Balts had separated into four distinct tribal cultures. The farming cultures of the Selonians and Semgallians were the smallest tribes and were generally peace-loving **agrarian** societies. The Couronians, on the west coast of the Baltic Sea, were a warlike society based on periodic invasion and looting of

The Vidzeme, a northeast section of Latvia, is perhaps the most diverse geographic region of Latvia, containing deep valleys and hills. The Siguldas pilsdrupas (Knights' Stonghold) pictured here was built at the beginning of the 13th century. It is one of many remnants of Latvia's proud history found in the area by the town of Sigulda.

other tribes. They became known as the "Vikings of the Baltic." The Latgallians, the largest tribe, had a fairly sophisticated society based on commerce and trade. These traders became prosperous via their profitable trade in Baltic amber, which was prized more highly than gold in some areas of Europe and the Near East. The Latgallians were the ancestors of modern Latvians.

THE CRUSADES AND GERMAN RULE

By the 1100s, Latvian lands had prospered through trade. Latvian merchants were doing business with Scandinavian, Russian, and Byzantine traders as well as new trading partners from Western Europe. By the late 1200s, Western Europe was the largest market for Latvian goods, and these merchants were eager to convert the **pagan** population of the Baltic region to Christianity.

The Baltic peoples had little interest in the new religion and were not about to give up centuries' worth of religious practices peacefully. In particular, the Baltic tribes were opposed to the Christian ritual of baptism. German merchants eventually brought home word of this opposition. When the news reached the Roman Catholic pope, he ordered Crusaders into the region to influence public opinion. These German crusaders, known as the Knights of the Sword (later known as the Livonian Order), forcibly converted the entire region by 1290. Riga, initially founded by German traders, became the center of the Baltic region and an important cultural crossroads between East and West.

The state that emerged under German rule was known as Livonia and encompassed modern-day Latvia and Estonia. A loose confederation of **feudal** states, Livonia became the center of the powerful Northern German Trading Organization, or Hanseatic League. The Hanseatic League was a major economic force of the period.

POLISH AND SWEDISH RULE

The Livonian War (1558–1583) resulted in the passage of Livonia's rule from German control to the Kingdom of Poland-Lithuania. For the average Livonian peasant, things changed little, since the landowning German nobility simply switched their allegiances to Poland in order to retain their lands and power.

The country became somewhat divided along religious lines at this point. Some areas with a strong German influence had accepted the Lutheran faith, while others remained staunchly Roman Catholic. The territory was ruled as a confederation of principalities and dukedoms, and some of these experienced a significant economic boom during the 1600s. In particular, the Dukedom of Kurzeme was economically thriving and even established two colonies—one on the Gambia River in Africa and one on the Caribbean island of Tobago. Both areas still retain some place names and other historical ties to their Baltic heritage.

Following the Polish-Swedish War (1600–1629), Livonia fell under Swedish control, with Riga now being the largest and most cosmopolitan Swedish city. During this time, the area became known as "Sweden's Bread Basket," because it supplied much of Sweden's population with wheat. During the years of Swedish rule, the last remaining cultural distinctions between the Baltic tribes disappeared. Couronians, Selonians, Semgallians, Livians, and Latgallians all began to identify themselves as Latvians, or in Latvian, the *Latviesi*. The concept of a nation as a culturally unified people that spoke one common language would prove to be an important idea in Latvian history, and its roots can be traced back to the Swedish period.

RUSSIAN RULE

By the 1700s, Russia had set its sights on expansion in hopes of securing a clear passage to Western Europe. The Great Northern War, between Sweden and Russia, was the result. By 1710, Czar Peter I had conquered the city of Vidzeme. From there, he staged his campaign for Riga, and by the end of the eighteenth century, all of Latvia was under Russian rule. Rich from its importance as a trading center, industry began to develop in the region, and the population swelled. By the end of the 1700s, Latvia had become one of Russia's richest and most industrially developed provinces.

The dawn of the nineteenth century marked a period of national awakening across Europe. The aggression of the French general Napoleon Bonaparte created a wave of **nationalism** that swept across the continent. The idea of a unified nation had great appeal to the Latvians, who had lived for centuries under foreign rule. Inspired by the renewed interest in national identity that was taking place among their neighbors to the west, the Latvian intellectual elite soon launched a national revival of their own.

Initial nationalist movements were limited to discussions of language, literature, and culture.

The Gutmana ala (Gutmanis Cave) bears the markings of thousands of visitors over the centuries who have carved names, initials, and insignia in the soft sand walls.

The first newspapers written in the Latvian language were published during this period, patriotic songs and poetry flourished, and active cultural development began to take place. The most active social and cultural leaders of this movement were called the "*jaunlatviesi*," or "new Latvians."

CHAPTER TWO—LATVIA'S HISTORY AND GOVERNMENT

Riga's skyline is filled with both new construction and old landmarks undergoing overdue renovations.

By 1900, the jaunlatviesi were no longer content with cultural and social reform. They now wanted political change. An independent and democratic Latvian state was the goal of these early nationalists, but it would take several more years and armed conflict before their hopes could be realized.

WORLD WAR I AND A BRIEF INDEPENDENCE

The inability of European leaders to ease political tensions between the different nationalities under their rule eventually led to war. World War I began on June 28, 1914, when Gavrilo Princip, a

EUROPEAN UNION—LATVIA

Serbian nationalist, assassinated Austrian archduke Franz Ferdinand and his wife, Sophie. Russia allied with Serbia. Germany sided with Austria and soon declared war on Russia. After France declared its support for Russia, Germany attacked France. German troops then invaded Belgium, a **neutral** country that stood between German forces and Paris. Great Britain then declared war on Germany.

The war devastated Latvia. As German troops advanced, Latvia became a battleground between German forces and the Soviet Red Army of Russia. More than half the Latvian population was forced to flee ahead of the German troops, and they became refugees in an inhospitable Soviet Union. The Red Army removed all important factory equipment, railroad equipment, and other valuables to the interior. None of these items would be returned after the war.

The Latvian nationalists saw their opportunity in the confusion that followed the end of World War I. As borders began to be redrawn across Europe, Latvia proclaimed its own independence on November 18, 1918. The first foreign country to recognize Latvian independence was the Soviet Union, on August 11, 1920. The Soviets recognized Latvian **autonomy** amid promises to relinquish authority over Latvian territory for all time. These promises would later prove false.

This first Latvian experiment with democracy ultimately failed. Internal economic difficulties created an unstable political situation, which made the country vulnerable to the ambitions of its powerful neighbors. However, this brief period of independence is still remembered with pride by Latvians, and November 18 is commemorated as Latvian Independence Day, marking the birth of the first truly Latvian nation.

WORLD WAR II AND THE END OF INDEPENDENCE

By 1933, Adolf Hitler had come to power in Germany. By 1938, he had occupied neighboring Austria as well. His stated objective was to unify all ethnic German peoples. He soon demanded the surrender of Czechoslovakia's Sudetenland, taking up the cause of the Sudeten Germans. On September 29, 1938, France, Germany, Italy, and Great Britain signed the Munich Agreement, demanding that Czechoslovakia surrender the Sudetenland to Germany in exchange for Hitler's promise of peace. However, in March 1939, Hitler reneged on his agreement and invaded the rest of Czechoslovakia, followed by an invasion of Poland. Well aware of Hitler's ambitious plans to conquer Europe, Soviet leader Josef Stalin negotiated the secret Molotov-Ribbentrop pact. This agreement pledged that Nazi Germany would not

Latvians have suffered over the centuries from soldiers from Germany and the Soviet Union. When Latvia was part of the USSR, however, monuments were erected praising Soviet forces for their role in liberating Latvia from the Nazis.

attack the Soviet Union; in return, the Soviets would not oppose further Nazi expansion.

This pact changed overnight the strategic value of the Baltic States. Latvia was now an area of interest to the USSR. On June 17, 1940, the Soviets orchestrated a communist uprising in all three Baltic nations. Once installed, these new communist governments requested membership in the Soviet Union, against the wishes of the majority of the people. A takeover of this magnitude could not be accomplished without some form of opposition, and so to eliminate dissent, the Soviets ordered the deportation of thousands of Latvian nationalists to Siberia. Most were taken away during the night of June 13, 1941.

As World War II progressed, Latvia was occupied by Nazi forces. During this time, 90 percent of Latvian Jews were murdered in Nazi concentration camps. Both the Russians and the Germans conscripted Latvian men for forced service in the army, causing devastating losses among a population with no real loyalty to either side.

By 1944, the Soviet Union had prevailed, and Latvia came under Soviet control once more. As a means to restore order and promote a "collective" mindset among the populace, the Soviets began an intensive program of **Russification.**

COMMUNIST RULE

The years immediately following World War II are still remembered with great sadness by the Latvian people. Many changes were forced on the Latvian people to **assimilate** them into the Russian-dominated culture of the Soviet Union. All government activity, including education, was now to be conducted in Russian. An estimated 120,000 Latvians suspected of having anti-Soviet political beliefs were imprisoned or deported to Siberia. Almost 130,000 Latvians fled to democratic countries in the West.

Latvia's agricultural system was overhauled to meet the requirements of central planners headquartered in Moscow. Smaller family farms that had operated successfully for decades were forced to join into large cooperative farms owned by the state. In March of 1949, another mass deportation took place. This time, 43,000 rural residents who opposed the state takeovers of private farms were deported to Siberia.

Latvia had been sparsely populated to begin with, and now it suffered a loss of manpower after the destruction of the war years and the series of deportations and defections during the early years of communist rule. Moscow solved the problem by importing great numbers of Russian laborers into the tiny country. At the beginning of World War II, more than 80 percent of Latvia was occupied by native Latvians. At the height of Russian immigration, Latvians comprised only 50 percent of the population, permanently altering the nation's cultural and linguistic landscape.

A RENEWED CRY FOR INDEPENDENCE

Soviet control of Latvia went unchallenged for many decades, in part because of harsh penalties

Outside of the cities, many Latvians still endure living standards that are low compared to European standards. Many hope that EU membership will mean greater economic development for the country.

imposed for dissent. The lasting power of communist rule was also rooted in the constant barrage of **propaganda** directed at the Baltic States. Because of their close cultural ties to the West, Communist Party leaders feared that the Latvian people would be seduced by the comparative wealth of nearby **capitalist** countries, such as Finland. State-owned Latvian television broadcast images of inner-city poverty, bag ladies, and race riots in the United States to help promote an image of the West as corrupt and dangerous.

By the 1980s, however, it was clear that these images and ideas were losing their power. Fueled by the success of anticommunist movements in

hand in hand. Forming a human chain that stretched from the capital cities of Tallinn, Estonia, through Riga, to Vilnius, Lithuania, the people of the Baltic States proclaimed themselves united in their wish for independence from Soviet rule.

On May 4, 1990, Latvia's first democratically elected parliament since the 1930s declared that Latvian independence from the Soviet Union would be reinstated after a brief transition period. August 21, 1991, marked the end of that transition period, and an independent Latvia was reborn. Soon after declaring its independence, Latvia joined the United Nations. Domestically, a series of sweeping reforms were implemented to bring Latvia out of the economic and political darkness that marked its decades as a communist state. By 2004, Latvia's most important foreign policy goals had been realized. On April 2, 2004, Latvia became a member of NATO, and on May 1, 2004, it was accepted as a member of the EU.

After centuries of foreign domination and conflict, Latvia has come a long way in its political and economic development. It is now a free and independent nation, looking forward to the future as an active member of the global community of nations.

other countries and the memory of an independent Latvia that had been destroyed by Soviet control, many different groups began to work toward the reinstatement of national independence. On August 23, 1989, fifty years after the signing of the infamous Molotov-Ribbentrop pact, thousands of Latvians, Lithuanians, and Estonians joined

Doma laukums, the main square of Riga, is bustling with diners and strollers during the summer evenings when the sun doesn't set until late.

3 THE ECONOMY

Latvia is emerging from a period of economic difficulty that marked its independence from Soviet control. Many challenges continue to face Latvia, although great strides have been made to implement a market economy that is competitive with the economies of greater Europe.

TRANSITION TO A MARKET ECONOMY

For much of the last century, Latvia's economy operated on the communist model. Under Soviet communism, all enterprise was owned by the state, and all economic policy was established in Moscow. This central planning was very ineffective since it did not take into account local needs or strengths. Also, by removing any sense of control from the local population, Latvians took little interest in developing new or more efficient means of production. Thus, when communism came to an end, the Latvian people were left with an **infrastructure** that was inadequate to compete in the world marketplace. Rapid reforms were needed to adapt to the rigors of a market economy.

The two main components of a market economy are **entrepreneurial** responsibility and competition. It is an entrepreneur's responsibility to see to her company's growth and to ensure that it can adapt to changing circumstances. Competition ensures that new products and technologies will constantly be developed as each business works to ensure that its product best meets the needs of the consumer. The government's role is limited to creating conditions favorable to a healthy economy by contributing to the infrastructure, as well as to fair labor and tax laws. The government also provides assistance to those unable to cope with the greater demands of a competitive market.

Making the change from a centrally planned economy to a market economy presents great challenges. Immediately following the collapse of the Soviet system, the Latvian economy experienced a number of major setbacks. Latvia suffered a major decrease in its exports, and many industries were unable to sell a large portion of their production. Energy prices skyrocketed, and unemployment reached an all-time high. Today, however, the situation has improved tremendously. In the mid-1990s, growth in the newly emerging **service sector** has helped to fuel a recovery. Unemployment has dropped, and foreign aid has helped rebuild the nation's deteriorating infrastructure. This paved the way for increased foreign investment. The Latvian economy has improved steadily and shown a pattern of consistent growth over the last five years.

THE NEW ECONOMY

Although one-quarter of Latvia's **gross domestic product (GDP)** comes from its manufacturing industries, the primary source of Latvia's income today comes from the service sector, which contributes nearly 70 percent of the country's GDP. This includes the country's wholesale and retail trade, transport, shipping, and storage, the emerging sectors of communications and **information technology**, and real estate management.

Latvia's banking system has also undergone systematic reform since the fall of communism. Today the Bank of Latvia is the major financial services provider in the country, and interest rates have stabilized enough to make credit cards and other forms of banking services more readily available.

INDUSTRY: A CRITICAL PIECE OF THE ECONOMY

Heavy industry is still an important part of Latvia's economy. Nearly a quarter of the country's GDP is dependent on the export of machines, electronics, and chemicals. Latvia also has many food and tex-

Riga's Central Market is one of Europe's largest and may be its most ancient. While it has moved over the years, the market dates from the city's founding in 1201.

Farming plays a larger role culturally than it does economically in Latvia.
Some people fear that EU membership could endanger Latvia's small farmers.

tile enterprises, and its forests provide wood for the manufacture of paper and building materials.

During the Soviet era, Latvia was the most industrialized of the Baltic States, and all diesel and electric trains produced for the Soviet Union were manufactured there. Other prominent Soviet era industries included the manufacture of buses, refrigeration equipment, and telephones. Following independence, many of these products could not compete with superior products being produced more efficiently in the West. Today, many of these factories are being updated to produce different products that are more competitive in world markets.

AGRICULTURE

Farms play a small but important role in the Latvian economy. Although it accounts for only about 5 percent of the GDP, agriculture is a growing area of the economy. Benefits of privatization in the agricultural sector are only beginning to be seen. Crops produced in Latvia include grain, sugar beets, potatoes, vegetables, beef, dairy products, eggs, and fish. A mounting concern after EU accession is the small size of most Latvian farms, many of which will not be large enough to receive EU subsidies without a significant investment. It is feared that the majority of small farmers, too poor to expand to the size necessary to meet EU quotas, will suffer as cheaper foodstuffs are imported from other EU nations.

ENERGY SOURCES

Imported fuel accounts for the majority of Latvia's energy supply. Wood and domestically produced electricity provide the remainder of Latvia's energy. Environmental protection and reducing dependence on foreign imports are among the most

The industrial center of Dauvgapils, Latvia's second largest city,
is an industrial center and also an important transit point for railroad transport.

important factors of Latvia's new, EU-driven energy policy; the nation hopes to secure EU funds for research into supplies of renewable energy. Energy research is taking place at universities and company labs all over the world, and Latvia does not want to be left behind. **Geothermal** energy sources, solar-power generation, hydro-electricity, and **biomass** research are some of the options being explored. Currently, hydroelectric power is the primary eco-friendly form of energy being utilized in Latvia. The country has no nuclear power facilities.

TRANSPORTATION AND COMMUNICATIONS

Highways, railways, waterways (both navigable rivers and seaports), and airports make up Latvia's transportation system. Transportation is critical to a competitive economy, so large investments are being made to update the nation's transportation system. Riga International Airport serves not only the other small national airports but hosts several international flights as well. The Via Baltica is a major international roadway, linking all three Baltic States with Scandinavia and Central Europe.

The communications infrastructure is also undergoing a period of dramatic change. Much additional investment is needed to connect the rural areas with basic telephone and television services. Plans are under way to upgrade the entire Latvian communication system and introduce an all-digital telephone network by the year 2012. Services such as Internet access and wireless telephone service are also being expanded but are currently available only in the most urban areas.

LOOKING AHEAD

As Latvia enters a new period of economic growth and begins to take advantage of the opportunities provided by its membership in the EU, the outlook for prosperity and an increased standard of living is bright. Challenges and much work remain, however, before Latvia is truly an equal partner with the more prosperous nations of the West.

Latvia is home to a variety of religious faiths. The church here was built by Old Believers, a small sect that rejected reforms of the Russian Orthodox Church initiated by Peter the Great.

4 LATVIA'S PEOPLE AND CULTURE

Latvia, a nation of less than three million people, has undergone important *demographic* changes since achieving independence in 1991. Already a small nation, the population has declined significantly. Primarily, this is due to the fact that there are currently more deaths than births in Latvia, people postponing the start of their families because of the economic uncertainty, and the region's already low birthrate.

Another critical factor has been the migration of non-Latvian peoples (predominantly ethnic Russians) to other countries. This is not only because of the economic difficulties faced in the postindependence period, but also because of the efforts to restore the Latvian culture that existed before Soviet occupation. The Latvian language has been reinstated as the official language of the country, even though it was eliminated from public education decades ago. Thirty-eight percent of the population belongs to a minority ethnic group. These minorities include Russians, Belorussians, Ukrainians, and Poles, who now feel as if they are suddenly living in a foreign country.

Important dialogues are taking place to reconcile the nation's ethnic diversity with the Latvians' need to reassert their cultural and national identity after decades of foreign domination.

QUICK FACTS: THE PEOPLE OF LATVIA

Population: 2,290,237
Ethnic groups: Latvian 57.7%, Russian 29.6%, Belorussian 4.1%, Ukrainian 2.7%, Polish 2.5%, Lithuanian 1.4%, other 2% (2002)
Age structure:
  0–14 years: 14.4%
  15–64 years: 69.4%
  65 years and over: 16.1%
Population growth rate: –0.69%
Birth rate: 9.04 births/1,000 pop.
Death rate: 13.7 deaths/1,000 pop.
Migration rate: –2.24 migrant(s)/1,000 pop.
Infant mortality rate: 9.55 deaths/1,000 live births
Life expectancy at birth:
  Total population: 71.05 years
  Male: 65.78 years
  Female: 76.6 years
Total fertility rate: 1.26 children born/woman
Religions: Lutheran, Roman Catholic, Russian Orthodox
Languages: Latvian (official), Lithuanian, Russian, other
Literacy rate: 99.8% (2003 est.)

Note: All figures are from 2005 estimates unless noted.
Source: www.cia.gov, 2005.

RELIGION: FREEDOM OF CHOICE

The Latvian people have full freedom to choose their faith and religion. Under communism, religious practices were discouraged if not completely outlawed. Since independence, a resurgence has been seen in the traditional Lutheran and Roman Catholic faiths, as well as in Russian Orthodoxy and less familiar religions from around the world. Baptists, Mormons, Pentecostals, Seventh-day Adventists, the Salvation Army, and even Buddhism and Hare Krishna have a presence in Latvia today.

Regina Aboltina, a resident of the eastern Latvian village of Subote, is proud of the religious diversity of her small town, which boasts four churches of different faiths, in addition to a synagogue.

Food and Drink: Simple Fare

The staples of Latvian cuisine are potatoes, cabbage, onions, other root vegetables, soups, mushrooms, poultry, red meat, and fish. Hearty dark breads made from whole grains are favorites here and may be served with cheese. Beverages are served at room temperature; cold drinks are considered unhealthy. American visitors are often surprised to see Latvians enjoying a nice *warm* Coca-Cola. Tapped birch juice is a popular national drink, as are various other brewed herbal beverages. Latvians produce their own national beer, and vodka is also popular.

Importance is placed on dining together as a family, a goal that is easily achieved since three generations of Latvian families often live together under the same roof. Breakfast usually consists of bread and butter served with tomatoes and ham or sausage. This is often accompanied by coffee or tea. Lunch, the main meal of the day, features soup with meat and potatoes. The evening meal is often little more than a snack, followed by dessert. This is usually eaten in the late evening.

Education: A Return to Traditional Studies

Latvians take education very seriously. Almost all adults can read and write, and most can speak at least two languages. In Latvia, education is **compulsory**, and every child between ages seven and sixteen must attend school. The school system, though, is quite different from most in North America. All Latvian children attend *Pamatskola*, or Basic School, until age sixteen. After Pamatskola, the students are divided into three different school streams. Some students go to *Arodpamatskola*, a two-year job-oriented school that concentrates on teaching practical skills. Others attend *Arodvidusskola*, which offers a broader general education. The remaining students enroll in the *Gimnazija*, the academic, college-preparatory school. Currently, the Latvian school system is undergoing major changes as it converts from a Russian-based educational program, implemented by the Soviets, to a more Western model taught in the Latvian language.

Sports: A Competitive People

Latvia is very proud of the accomplishments of its athletes. In particular, the country has a distinguished history of Olympic accomplishments. Latvia was a proud participant in the earliest twentieth-century Olympic competitions and had many independent sports clubs and organizations to promote the development of Latvian athletes. Unfortunately, all the organizations were banned under Soviet occupation. Because of their prominence as public figures, many important

Latvian athletes of the 1940s were deported to Siberia. Most of these died under the harsh conditions in the Soviet *gulags*.

Inspired by the loss of this important part of their culture, Latvians have rushed to embrace competitive sports since independence. Physical education is compulsory for all Latvian schoolchildren, and "Sports for All" has become a popular slogan, promoting the importance of competitive sports for Latvians of all ages. Latvia has participated in all Olympic Games held since achieving independence in 1991, and the success of Igors Vihrovs, who won the Gold Medal for Floor Exercise at the Sydney Games in 2000, has inspired the small nation.

While Latvian cookery is known for using basic ingredients such as cabbage, potatoes and onions, fine desserts can also be obtained, as proven by this chocolate torte served in a Riga restaurant.

Music of all sorts can be heard in the streets of Riga, from traditional folk music to bossa nova played by a saxophonist outside St. Peter's Church.

MUSIC: CULTURAL IDENTITY THROUGH SONG

Latvia is home to a unique art form known as the *Daina*. This traditional folk music has played a critical role in preserving the language, culture, and history of the Latvian people.

More than just a widely recognized song sung to a familiar melody, the Daina has very specific musical elements that distinguish it from other forms of music. Formally defined as a song sung in quatrain whose lyrics are specifically Latvian in structure and content, many of these songs have been passed down as an oral tradition for more than a thousand years. Popular themes are farming, marriage and love, pregnancy, childbirth, aging, and death.

Very specific songs are sung to mark religious occasions such as baptisms, weddings, and funerals. Another unique feature of the Daina is its focus on daily life from a woman's perspective. For example, drinking songs underscore the potential suffering of a drunk's wife and children. War songs do not glorify bravery and death but rather emphasize the loss suffered by those left behind. More than a million Daina texts have been identified, sung to more than thirty thousand traditional melodies. Still an important part of Latvian life, the country's people are very proud of this unique art form.

Riga plays a dominant role in the cultural and political life of Latvia. Looking southwest from the highest building in Riga, the Hotel Reval, the flat plain stretches past the Daugava River.

5 THE CITIES

Latvia was the most urbanized of the Baltic States under Soviet control. However, since achieving independence in 1991, a shift has been seen as more and more people migrate to rural areas to take advantage of the privatization of formerly state-owned farms. A majority of Latvians still live around urban centers. These are not large metropolises like London, Paris, or

While Riga is known for its baroque and Art Nouveau architecture, the city has also embraced modern movements as well, as entrepreneurs compete in a developing economy.

Rome, but rather small cities where jobs are more readily available. As a result, even the cities in Latvia retain a certain amount of rural character.

RIGA: THE CAPITAL

Riga is Latvia's capital and most populated city. Founded in 1201, it is also the country's oldest city and has been an important center for trade for centuries. Riga sits on the Daugava River, near the Bay of Riga on the Baltic Sea, and is an important merchant port as well as the nation's largest industrial center.

As a city that has survived for more than eight hundred years, it is not surprising that Riga boasts a host of important historical sites. While still retaining the character of a walled, medieval town, Riga is a showcase of impressive architecture in a great variety of styles that include Romanesque, Gothic, Baroque, Classicism, Eclecticism, and Art Nouveaux. On the outskirts of the city, old wooden homes provide a glimpse into the traditional building styles of the Latvian working classes. The design of these wooden structures has remained much the same since feudal times.

Riga is also the home of Latvia's cultural life. With twenty-eight museums, seven professional theaters, twelve cinemas, four concert halls, and a zoo, an important cultural or educational event is always taking place. The city is home to nearly three hundred different amateur art and performance groups. Riga is also the nation's educational center, with fourteen public and nine private colleges and universities. Since independence, Latvia has worked to bring attention to Riga's virtues as a tourist attraction, and tourism has increased dramatically, as thousands of tourists from around the world come to experience the many wonders of this ancient city.

DAUGAVPILS: A RICH METROPOLIS

Latvia's second-most populated city, Daugavpils, is an important industrial center. Its location on the Daugava River, combined with its proximity to Latvia's borders with Belarus, Lithuania, and Russia, has made it a hub for commercial storage and transport. Now celebrating its seven hundred and thirtieth anniversary as a city, Daugavpils is also home to a number of important historical and architectural sites. The most prominent is the Daugavpils Fortress, built in the eighteenth century. The city is also home to the nation's largest teacher's college, an important theater, and other smaller cultural institutions. The surrounding area is dotted with picturesque lakes, making the area an ideal tourist destination. Daugavpils is investing heavily in marketing itself as an international tourist attraction.

LIEPAJA AND VENTSPILS: IMPORTANT SEAPORTS

Located to the west of the capital city of Riga, Liepaja and Ventspils are port cities, located directly on the coast of the Baltic Sea. Home to fishing industries, commercial shipping, and manufacturing and textile enterprises, these cities are important economic centers for Latvia.

First established in 1253, Liepaja has an ancient history as a trade center. Many important architectural sites are located here, including churches built in different historical styles. Like the rest of Latvia, Liepaja has changed hands many times over the centuries, and traces of the various dominating cultures can be found throughout the ancient city.

Ventspils is also very old, having recently celebrated its seven hundredth anniversary. As the celebration approached, city leaders formed a plan to restore the city to its former glory, and the results have been spectacular. Many neglected historic buildings and monuments have been restored. One of the most important is the historic castle built by the German knights of the Livonian Order, which now houses a museum. Roads have been repaved, and bus, rail, and ferry services have been updated. New construction projects include the nation's only amusement park and a modern stadium complex.

EUROPEAN UNION—LATVIA

Visitors expecting a quiet Baltic scene will be surprised by the hustle and bustle evident on Riga's streets.

Trade has long been important to the Latvian economy.
Many of the fresh fruits in its markets for example, are grown far from the Baltic region.

VALMIERA: AN INDUSTRIAL HUB

At the crossroads of several important motorways, Valmiera is another important Latvian industrial center. Established as early as 1280, when knights of the Livonian Order chose the spot on the banks of the Gauja River to build a castle and a Catholic church, the city has a long and rich history. Unfortunately, Valmiera suffered a devastating fire in 1702, and many of its oldest buildings were lost. Today, Valmiera is home to many important industries, including dairy, grain, and meat processing, fiberglass production, metalworking, wood processing, paper production, and furniture manufacture.

The EU flag

6

THE FORMATION OF THE EUROPEAN UNION

The EU is an economic and political confederation of twenty-five European nations. Member countries abide by common foreign and security policies and cooperate on judicial and domestic affairs. The confederation, however, does not replace existing states or governments. Each of the twenty-five member states is **autonomous**, but they have all agreed to establish some common institutions and to hand over some of their own decision-making powers to these international bodies. As a result, decisions on matters that interest all member states can be made democratically, accommodating everyone's concerns and interests.

Today, the EU is the most powerful regional organization in the world. It has evolved from a primarily economic organization to an increasingly political one. Besides promoting economic cooperation, the EU requires that its members uphold fundamental values of peace and **solidarity**, human dignity, freedom, and equality. Based on the principles of democracy and the rule of law, the EU respects the culture and organizations of member states.

HISTORY

The seeds of the EU were planted more than fifty years ago in a Europe reduced to smoking piles of rubble by two world wars. European nations suffered great financial difficulties in the postwar period. They were struggling to get back on their feet and realized that another war would cause further hardship. Knowing that internal conflict was hurting all of Europe, a drive began toward European cooperation.

France took the first historic step. On May 9, 1950 (now celebrated as Europe Day), Robert Schuman, the French foreign minister, proposed the coal and steel industries of France and West Germany be coordinated under a single supranational authority. The proposal, known as the Treaty

of Paris, attracted four other countries—Belgium, Luxembourg, the Netherlands, and Italy—and resulted in the 1951 formation of the European Coal and Steel Community (ECSC). These six countries became the founding members of the EU.

In 1957, European cooperation took its next big leap. Under the Treaty of Rome, the European Economic Community (EEC) and the European Atomic Energy Community (EURATOM) were formed. Informally known as the Common Market, the EEC promoted joining the national economies into a single European economy. The 1965 Treaty of Brussels (more commonly referred to as the Merger Treaty) united these various treaty organizations under a single umbrella, the European Community (EC).

In 1992, the Maastricht Treaty (also known as the Treaty of the European Union) was signed in Maastricht, the Netherlands, signaling the birth of the EU as it stands today. **Ratified** the following year, the Maastricht Treaty provided for a central banking system, a common currency (the euro) to replace the national currencies, a legal definition of the EU, and a framework for expanding the

The EU's united economy has allowed it to become a worldwide financial power.

EU's political role, particularly in the area of foreign and security policy.

By 1993, the member countries completed their move toward a single market and agreed to participate in a larger common market, the European Economic Area, established in 1994.

The EU, headquartered in Brussels, Belgium, reached its current member strength in spurts. In

© BCE ECB EZB EKT EKP 2002

© BCE ECB EZB EKT EKP 2002

© BCE ECB EZB EKT EKP 2002

© BCE ECB EZB EKT EKP 2002

The euro, the EU's currency

1973, Denmark, Ireland, and the United Kingdom joined the six founding members of the EC. They were followed by Greece in 1981, and Portugal and Spain in 1986. The 1990s saw the unification of the two Germanys, and as a result, East Germany entered the EU fold. Austria, Finland, and Sweden joined the EU in 1995, bringing the total number of member states to fifteen. In 2004, the EU nearly doubled its size when ten countries—Cyprus, the Czech Republic, Estonia, Hungary, Latvia, Lithuania, Malta, Poland, Slovakia, and Slovenia—became members.

THE EU FRAMEWORK

The EU's structure has often been compared to a "roof of a temple with three columns." As established by the Maastricht Treaty, this three-pillar framework encompasses all the policy areas—or pillars—of European cooperation. The three pillars of the EU are the European Community, the Common Foreign and Security Policy (CFSP), and Police and Judicial Co-operation in Criminal Matters.

QUICK FACTS: THE EUROPEAN UNION

Number of Member Countries: 25

Official Languages: 20—Czech, Danish, Dutch, English, Estonian, Finnish, French, German, Greek, Hungarian, Italian, Latvian, Lithuanian, Maltese, Polish, Portuguese, Slovak, Slovenian, Spanish, and Swedish; additional language for treaty purposes: Irish Gaelic

Motto: *In Varietate Concordia* (United in Diversity)

European Council's President: Each member state takes a turn to lead the council's activities for 6 months.

European Commission's President: José Manuel Barroso (Portugal)

European Parliament's President: Josep Borrell (Spain)

Total Area: 1,502,966 square miles (3,892,685 sq. km.)

Population: 454,900,000

Population Density: 302.7 people/square mile (116.8 people/sq. km.)

GDP: €9.61.1012

Per Capita GDP: €21,125

Formation:
- Declared: February 7, 1992, with signing of the Maastricht Treaty
- Recognized: November 1, 1993, with the ratification of the Maastricht Treaty

Community Currency: Euro. Currently 12 of the 25 member states have adopted the euro as their currency.

Anthem: "Ode to Joy"

Flag: Blue background with 12 gold stars arranged in a circle

Official Day: Europe Day, May 9

Source: europa.eu.int

PILLAR ONE

The European Community pillar deals with economic, social, and environmental policies. It is a body consisting of the European Parliament, European Commission, European Court of Justice, Council of the European Union, and the European Courts of Auditors.

PILLAR TWO

The idea that the EU should speak with one voice in world affairs is as old as the European integration process itself. Toward this end, the Common Foreign and Security Policy (CFSP) was formed in 1993.

PILLAR THREE

The cooperation of EU member states in judicial and criminal matters ensures that its citizens enjoy the freedom to travel, work, and live securely and safely anywhere within the EU. The third pillar—Police and Judicial Co-operation in Criminal Matters—helps to protect EU citizens from international crime and to ensure equal access to justice and fundamental rights across the EU.

The flags of the EU's nations:

top row, left to right
Belgium, the Czech Republic, Denmark, Germany, Estonia, Greece

second row, left to right
Spain, France, Ireland, Italy, Cyprus, Latvia

third row, left to right
Lithuania, Luxembourg, Hungary, Malta, the Netherlands, Austria

bottom row, left to right
Poland, Portugal, Slovenia, Slovakia, Finland, Sweden, United Kingdom

ECONOMIC STATUS

As of May 2004, the EU had the largest economy in the world, followed closely by the United States. But even though the EU continues to enjoy a trade surplus, it faces the twin problems of high unemployment rates and ***stagnancy***.

The 2004 addition of ten new member states is expected to boost economic growth. EU membership is likely to stimulate the economies of these relatively poor countries. In turn, their prosperity growth will be beneficial to the EU.

THE EURO

The EU's official currency is the euro, which came into circulation on January 1, 2002. The shift to the euro has been the largest monetary changeover in the world. Twelve countries—Belgium, Germany, Greece, Spain, France, Ireland, Italy, Luxembourg, the Netherlands, Finland, Portugal, and Austria—have adopted it as their currency.

SINGLE MARKET

Within the EU, laws of member states are harmonized and domestic policies are coordinated to create a larger, more-efficient single market.

The chief features of the EU's internal policy on the single market are:

- free trade of goods and services

- a common EU competition law that controls anticompetitive activities of companies and member states

- removal of internal border control and harmonization of external controls between member states

- freedom for citizens to live and work anywhere in the EU as long as they are not dependent on the state

- free movement of **capital** between member states

- harmonization of government regulations, corporation law, and trademark registration

- a single currency

- coordination of environmental policy

- a common agricultural policy and a common fisheries policy

- a common system of indirect taxation, the value-added tax (VAT), and common customs duties and **excise**

- funding for research

- funding for aid to disadvantaged regions

The EU's external policy on the single market specifies:

- a common external **tariff** and a common position in international trade negotiations

- funding of programs in other Eastern European countries and developing countries

COOPERATION AREAS

EU member states cooperate in other areas as well. Member states can vote in European Parliament elections. Intelligence sharing and cooperation in criminal matters are carried out through EUROPOL and the Schengen Information System.

The EU is working to develop common foreign and security policies. Many member states are resisting such a move, however, saying these are sensitive areas best left to individual member states. Arguing in favor of a common approach to security and foreign policy are countries like France and Germany, who insist that a safer and more secure Europe can only become a reality under the EU umbrella.

One of the EU's great achievements has been to create a boundary-free area within which people, goods, services, and money can move around freely; this ease of movement is sometimes called "the four freedoms." As the EU grows in size, so do the challenges facing it—and yet its fifty-year history has amply demonstrated the power of cooperation.

Europe is proud of its "bright idea," a union with economic and political power.

The EU believes that it can use its power to act as a "lighthouse" for the rest of the world.

KEY EU INSTITUTIONS

Five key institutions play a specific role in the EU.

THE EUROPEAN PARLIAMENT

The European Parliament (EP) is the democratic voice of the people of Europe. Directly elected every five years, the Members of the European Parliament (MEPs) sit not in national **blocs** but in political groups representing the seven main political parties of the member states. Each group reflects the political ideology of the national parties to which its members belong. Some MEPs are not attached to any political group.

COUNCIL OF THE EUROPEAN UNION

The Council of the European Union (formerly known as the Council of Ministers) is the main leg-

islative and decision-making body in the EU. It brings together the nationally elected representatives of the member-state governments. One minister from each of the EU's member states attends council meetings. It is the forum in which government representatives can assert their interests and reach compromises. Increasingly, the Council of the European Union and the EP are acting together as colegislators in decision-making processes.

EUROPEAN COMMISSION

The European Commission does much of the day-to-day work of the EU. Politically independent, the commission represents the interests of the EU as a whole, rather than those of individual member states. It drafts proposals for new European laws, which it presents to the EP and the Council of the European Union. The European Commission makes sure EU decisions are implemented properly and supervises the way EU funds are spent. It also sees that everyone abides by the European treaties and European law.

The EU member-state governments choose the European Commission president, who is then approved by the EP. Member states, in consultation with the incoming president, nominate the other European Commission members, who must also be approved by the EP. The commission is appointed for a five-year term, but can be dismissed by the EP. Many members of its staff work in Brussels, Belgium.

COURT OF JUSTICE

Headquartered in Luxembourg, the Court of Justice of the European Communities consists of one independent judge from each EU country. This court ensures that the common rules decided in the EU are understood and followed uniformly by all the members. The Court of Justice settles disputes over how EU treaties and legislation are interpreted. If national courts are in doubt about how to apply EU rules, they must ask the Court of Justice. Individuals can also bring proceedings against EU institutions before the court.

COURT OF AUDITORS

EU funds must be used legally, economically, and for their intended purpose. The Court of Auditors, an independent EU institution located in Luxembourg, is responsible for overseeing how EU money is spent. In effect, these auditors help European taxpayers get better value for the money that has been channeled into the EU.

OTHER IMPORTANT BODIES

1. European Economic and Social Committee: expresses the opinions of organized civil society on economic and social issues

2. Committee of the Regions: expresses the opinions of regional and local authorities

3. European Central Bank: responsible for monetary policy and managing the euro

4. European Ombudsman: deals with citizens' complaints about mismanagement by any EU institution or body

5. European Investment Bank: helps achieve EU objectives by financing investment projects

Together with a number of agencies and other bodies completing the system, the EU's institutions have made it the most powerful organization in the world.

EU Member States

In order to become a member of the EU, a country must have a stable democracy that guarantees the rule of law, human rights, and protection of minorities. It must also have a functioning market economy as well as a civil service capable of applying and managing EU laws.

The EU provides substantial financial assistance and advice to help candidate countries prepare themselves for membership. As of October 2004, the EU has twenty-five member states. Bulgaria and Romania are likely to join in 2007, which would bring the EU's total population to nearly 500 million.

In December 2004, the EU decided to open negotiations with Turkey on its proposed membership. Turkey's possible entry into the EU has been fraught with controversy. Much of this controversy has centered on Turkey's human rights record and the divided island of Cyprus. If allowed to join the EU, Turkey would be its most-populous member state.

The 2004 expansion was the EU's most ambitious enlargement to date. Never before has the EU embraced so many new countries, grown so much in terms of area and population, or encompassed so many different histories and cultures. As the EU moves forward into the twenty-first century, it will undoubtedly continue to grow in both political and economic strength.

The City Canal of Riga provides an opportunity for recreation and relaxation.

7 LATVIA IN THE EUROPEAN UNION

Ten new member nations were admitted to the EU in 2004: Latvia, Cyprus, Estonia, Hungary, Slovakia, Lithuania, Malta, Poland, the Czech Republic, and Slovenia. As a relatively new member of the EU, Latvia is undergoing a critical period of growth as it adjusts to the new economic and political situation.

LATVIA AND EU ACCESSION

In the wake of the collapse of the Soviet Union, Latvia faced many economic and political challenges. Having always identified themselves more with the nations of Western Europe than with Russia in the east, Latvians were eager to restore what they saw as traditional ties with their neighbors in the West. Membership in NATO and the EU became Latvia's top foreign policy priorities.

In 2003, following a transition period of sweeping economic and political reforms, Latvians voted for membership in the EU in a historic **referendum**. Although national polls showed that some Latvians had concerns about joining the EU, the majority felt that tapping into the resources of a wider Europe would bring their new country more advantages than disadvantages. The process of joining the EU, called **accession**, requires potential member states to adopt common policies on a wide variety of issues—from trade and commerce to environmental protection and human rights.

DIFFERING VIEWS OF A UNITED EUROPE

Public opinion in Europe remains divided about the amount of decision-making control member nations should give to the EU. Most Latvians want to surrender a minimum of **sovereignty**, especially over such things as defense and foreign policy. Concern has been expressed that as a nation that has only recently gained a democratically elected legislative body, the Latvian voting public should have more control over legislation being passed than the European Parliament in Brussels. Currently Latvia and many of the other new EU states support a policy termed intergovernmentalism—a governmental approach in which member states must decide on policy by unanimous agreement. Latvians remain concerned that their status as a new member of the EU, combined with their relative economic weakness, puts their interests behind those of larger countries like Germany in EU decision making.

Meanwhile, other Europeans, primarily in the larger EU countries, feel strongly that the greatest opportunities for growth can be found within the framework of a strongly united Europe. Supporters of supranationalism—a governmental approach in which EU member states would be bound by decisions based on majority rule, believe that the benefits of having common policies for defense, treaty negotiation, and trade far outweigh the individual interests of separate member states.

BENEFITS OF EU MEMBERSHIP

EU membership is expected to have a tremendous impact on the standard of living in many parts of Latvia.

For example, great discrepancies exist between the standard of living enjoyed by urban Latvians, such as those living in Riga, as compared to the conditions faced by poorer citizens in the more rural areas of the country. Many of the roadways are still suffering from decades of neg-

The House of Blackheads housed a merchants' guild after it was constructed in the mid-fourteenth century. The building was destroyed during World War II, and its ruins razed by the Soviets. In 2001, however, a striking reconstruction of the original building was opened, a testament to Latvia's pride in its heritage.

lect that originated during the Soviet era. This complicates the commercial transport of goods and services.

As a new member of the EU, Latvia will be able to access millions of dollars in additional funding to develop an infrastructure that is comparable to the rest of Europe. The funds are allocated to help address the economic and social inequalities between the richest and poorest EU nations. This money will be used to support agriculture, build new roads and bridges, develop health-care and social welfare programs, and improve environmental conditions. All these improvements are designed to promote continued foreign investment.

With the financial assistance the Latvians receive from the EU helping to create a favorable business environment, Latvia will be able to lower its corporate taxes in hopes of luring companies away from areas where it is more expensive to do business. The potential of economic assistance to help level the playing field between Latvia and its neighbors to the west was one of the strongest motivating factors behind the decision to move forward with EU accession.

Latvia can also apply to the EU for millions in research dollars. The EU is a large source of fund-

Some Latvians are uncertainly walking into the future, as they contemplate the imminent membership in the European Union.

ing for all types of scientific investigation. Large sums of money are available to promote the development of **sustainable** agriculture, alternative energy sources, and medicine.

AREAS OF CONCERN

Although Latvia has much to gain by its membership in the EU, lingering concerns persist that not all areas of society will benefit from membership. One element of EU membership that was once perceived to be a great benefit to Latvian workers was the free movement of labor. In theory, workers from one EU country could move to another EU member nation to find work without having to go through normal immigration procedures. For many unemployed or low-earning workers, the possibility of relocating freely to neighboring states with higher wages and better standards of living was very appealing, especially for those Latvian citizens of minority backgrounds who sought to leave the country anyway.

Unfortunately for Latvian workers, and workers from the other nine new EU states, the prospect of a flood of workers from poor Eastern European nations was threatening to many of the richer nations of the EU. For example, many large European nations, like France and Germany, support large and expensive social welfare programs that give financial assistance, housing, and health care to their poor. The fear that waves of poor laborers will move in and drain the economies of these larger nations from millions in welfare dollars has caused most of the

older EU countries to restrict the movement of labor to needed professionals.

Another segment of the Latvian population which may not benefit from EU accession is the country's thousands of small farmers. Shortly after achieving independence, Latvia implemented programs to privatize the country's large collective farms. Many young Latvians, unhappy with factory work, took advantage of government incentives to relocate to rural areas and farm. Unfortunately, many of these farmers cannot meet the large quotas required to receive farm subsidies from the EU under their CAP program. As a result, these small farmers fear they will lose local buyers for their products as produce from other EU nations makes its way to Latvian markets. These products will likely be less expensive than locally grown products due to the subsidies received by these larger farms in other areas of the EU. Only time will tell if these fears will be realized.

LOOKING FORWARD

While a few concerns over their sovereignty and national interests remain, there is little doubt that the EU will greatly improve the standard of living, economic security, and prominence of Latvia on the world stage. The availability of EU funds for building a more stable infrastructure and a favorable climate for foreign investment is helping to drive a steady recovery from the poverty that marked its years as a communist state. The few drawbacks to Latvian membership in the EU are far outweighed by the potential benefits.

A Calendar of Latvian Festivals

Latvia celebrates many important holidays and days of remembrance. These celebrations are usually religious in nature or they relate to an important event in Latvian history.

January: January 1 is a public holiday. The **New Year** festivities traditionally include champagne and fireworks. January 20 is **Commemoration of Defenders of the Barricades Day**. In January 1991, Soviet leaders briefly decided to oppose Latvian independence and sent special forces troops to secure the Ministry of the Interior. People from all over Latvia rushed to Riga to build barricades and repel the attack. Although hostilities lasted for only a few days, several people were killed and Latvians honor their sacrifice on this day. January 26 celebrates the **International Recognition of the Republic of Latvia**.

March/April: Easter Week may fall in March or April, and the festival is celebrated throughout the country. In Latvia, **Easter** festivities often last for three days. March 25 marks **Commemoration Day of Victims of Communist Terror**. This day is a day to remember the thousands of innocent Latvians who were forcibly deported and imprisoned in the early days of the Soviet occupation.

May: May 1 is **Labor Day**, since the fall of communism this day has been celebrated as a day of rest from work. May 4 is **Independence Day**, and celebrates Latvian independence. **Mother's Day** is celebrated on the second Sunday in May each year. May 8 is the **Crushing of Nazism and Commemoration Day for the Victims of World War II**. As one would guess, this is a day to remember those killed during World War II. In Latvia, they also grieve for the thousands of Latvian men and boys forcibly conscripted to fight by both sides. Nearly 100,000 of these conscripted soldiers died in battle.

June: June 23 and 24 are celebrated as **Ligo** and **Jani**. These festivals date back to pagan times and celebrate the summer solstice. This celebration is always met with great joy as it marks the return of summer and its longer days after many months of darkness. Festivities include decorating houses and livestock with massive bouquets of wildflowers, and the singing of special Dainas. Special Jani cheese is made for the occasion and is served with barley beer. June 22 is **Heroes Commemoration Day**. This day marks the Battle of Cesis, when troops from the newly independent Latvian Republic repelled an attack by German troops.

July: July 4 marks **Commemoration Day of Genocide Against the Jews**. This day remembers all of the victims of the Nazi Holocaust. The date was chosen because on July 4, 1941, Nazi forces burned Riga's main Jewish synagogue to the ground. Most of the city's Jewish inhabitants were locked inside.

August: August 11 is the **Commemoration Day of Latvian Freedom Fighters**, which celebrates Soviet acceptance of an independent Latvia in 1920. This acceptance came after a series of military skirmishes between Latvian fighters and Soviet troops. August 21 is **Constitution Day** and marks the complete restoration of Latvian Independence in 1991.

September: Baltic Unity Day on September 22 celebrates the victory of united Latvian and Lithuanian forces against German crusaders in 1236.

November: Proclamation of the Republic of Latvia on November 18 is an important day marking the declaration of Latvian Independence that took place after World War I on this date in 1918. **All Souls Day**, celebrated on the last Sunday of November, is a day to remember the dead, and family members light candles of remembrance at the graves of loved ones.

December: The first Sunday of December is the **Commemoration Day of the Victims of Genocide Against the Latvian People by the Totalitarian Communist Regime**. A different holiday than that observed on March 25, this holiday recognizes the 70,000 Latvians who were living in interior regions of the Soviet Union following World War I. Forced to flee in advance of the invading German forces, these Latvian citizens became refugees in the Soviet Union and were not permitted to return to the newly independent Latvia following the war. They were exterminated by Soviet ruler Josef Stalin between 1937 and 1938.

    Christmas festivities take place on December 24, 25, and 26. Families gather to decorate the tree on Christmas Eve and attend church services. The following days are marked by family feasts, music, and gift giving. **New Year's Eve** celebrations get started at nightfall on December 31, and often last well into the next morning.

Paska (Molded Cheese Dessert)

This traditional dish is a favorite dessert across Latvia. Although traditionally molded into the shape of a pyramid, Western cooks will probably find a Jello mold suitable.

Ingredients
1 pint cottage cheese
4 hard-boiled egg yolks
3/4 cups sugar
1/2 stick butter
1/2 teaspoon vanilla
1 teaspoon orange peel
1/2 cup currants (or raisins if no currants are available)
1/4 cup ground walnuts
cheesecloth

Directions
Combine the first five ingredients in a blender or mixer and beat until smooth. Stir in remaining ingredients. Poke a hole in the bottom of the mold for drainage, and line the mold with dampened cheesecloth. Pour in the cheese mixture. Place the entire mold in a large pan to catch the drippings. Refrigerate for 48 to 72 hours and discard any liquid that drains out of the mold. Remove the cheese by overturning the mold onto a large, decorative plate and lifting the edges of the cheesecloth. Serve immediately.

Latvian Herring Salad

This is a traditional main dish and a staple of the Latvian diet.

Ingredients
1 jar pickled herring
1 Granny Smith apple, finely diced
3 hard-boiled eggs, diced
4 large dill pickles, diced
1/4 cup mayonnaise
1/4 cup whipping cream
1 teaspoon curry powder

Directions
Drain the herring and rinse. Dice herring and mix with remaining ingredients. Chill before serving.

Piragi

This side dish is a Latvian favorite.

Ingredients
2 cans sauerkraut
1 medium onion, diced
1/2 stick butter
2 tablespoons brown sugar
1 teaspoon caraway seeds
2 thick slices of bacon

Directions
Open the first can of sauerkraut into a colander and rinse well. Melt the butter in a large frying pan and sauté the onions until soft. Push the onions to the side of the pan. Add the brown sugar to the pan and when it starts to bubble push the onions back into the center of the pan and coat with the melted sugar. Add the rinsed sauerkraut. Open the second can of sauerkraut and drain but do not rinse. Add this sauerkraut to the pan and mix well. Transfer the entire mixture to a large baking dish. Add 3/4 cup of water to the hot frying pan and scrape the drippings off the bottom. Bring water to a boil and add caraway seeds. Remove from heat and pour over sauerkraut in the baking dish. Top with bacon strips and cover. Bake at 350° for an hour and a half.

Latvian Beet Soup

Serves 8–12

Ingredients
6–8 large, fresh beets, 14–16 medium-sized
    ones, or 24 tiny new ones
1–2 handfuls of rolled oats (or rice)
6–8 medium-sized potatoes
3–4 beef bouillon cubes
chopped hard-boiled eggs (1 per serving)
sour cream (1 ounce per serving)

Directions
Wash beets well, and cut off the roots leaving about an inch of the greens. Place beets and enough water to cover into a large Dutch oven or stockpot. Bring to a boil, and cook until beets are soft, about 10–20 minutes, depending on the size of the beets. When soft, drain off the water and set aside to cool. After cooling, peel.

Peel then dice the potatoes into 1/2-inch chunks. In a large pot, put 2 1/2 quarts of water. Add the bouillon cubes, oats or rice, and the diced potatoes. Bring to a boil, then simmer covered until the potatoes are fork soft.

Meanwhile, put the cooled beets into a food processor or blender and puree until the desired consistency. Add to the potato mixture and stir well. Simmer until the beets are heated through.

When ready to serve, place a dollop of sour cream and 1 chopped hard-boiled egg into each soup bowl. Fill with soup.

Latvian Apple Loaf

Ingredients
5 ounces butter
1/2 cup sugar
3 eggs, separated
1 cup flour
2 teaspoons baking powder
2 teaspoons vanilla
3 tablespoons milk or cream
6 medium apples, peeled and thickly sliced
(Granny Smith or Macintosh are best)
1/4 cup chopped walnuts (optional)
1 tablespoon sugar mixed with 1/4 teaspoon
cinnamon

Directions
Preheat oven to 375°F. Lightly butter a loaf pan.
Sift flour with the baking powder into a medium-
sized bowl. Set aside.

With a mixer on high, cream together butter and sugar into a large bowl, adding the sugar a little at a time. Add egg yolks one at a time to butter mixture, beating well after each addition. Add vanilla.

Add the flour mixture to the butter in 2 or 3 parts, alternating them with the milk. Add the walnuts if using. In a small, clean, bowl, whip the egg whites until they form stiff peaks. Gently fold the egg whites into the batter. Pour the batter into the loaf pan, and press the apple slices deep into the batter. Sprinkle with the sugar and cinnamon mixture.

Bake 30–50 minutes, or until tester inserted in the middle comes out dry.

PROJECT AND REPORT IDEAS

Maps

- Make a map of the eurozone, and create a legend to indicate key manufacturing industries throughout the EU.
- Create a map of Latvia using a legend to represent all the major products produced there. The map should clearly indicate all of the cities mentioned in this book.

Reports

- Write a brief report on Latvia's seaports.
- Many of Latvia's industries today were centrally planned by Moscow during the communist era. Write a report discussing the advantages and disadvantages of this situation. How does it affect the products produced in Latvia today?
- Write a report on Latvia's concerns within the EU.
- Write a brief report on any of the following historical events: World War I, World War II, the movement for Latvian independence.

Journal

- Imagine you are an ethnic Russian living in Latvia today. What things about your life have changed, what things have stayed the same? Write a journal about your experience and discuss whether you will stay in Latvia or move elsewhere.
- Read more about Latvia's cities and culture. Plan a vacation in Latvia and write a journal describing your travels and the places you visited.

Projects

- Learn the Latvian expressions for simple words such as hello, good day, please, thank you. Try them on your friends.
- Make a calendar of your country's festivals and list the ones that are common or similar in Latvia. Are they celebrated differently in Latvia? If so, how?

- Go online or to the library and find images of medieval fortresses. Create a model of one.
- Make a protest poster demonstrating for Latvian independence.
- Make a list of all the places that you have read about in this book and indicate them on a map of Latvia.
- Find a Latvian recipe other than the ones given in this book, and ask an adult to help you make it. Share it with members of your class.
- Read a few examples of Dainas and create your own.

Group Activities

- Debate: One side should take the role of Germany and the other Latvia. Germany's position is that EU should adopt a supranational approach, while Latvia will speak in favor of the intergovernmental mode.
- Role play: Reenact the scene at the defense of the barricades in 1991 as Latvians from all over the country came to Riga to stand against Soviet troops.

CHRONOLOGY

9000 BCE	Arrival of Latvia's earliest inhabitants, after the withdrawal of the glaciers.
2000 BCE	Baltic tribes (ancestors of modern Latvians) first settle the territory.
900 CE	Baltic tribes form four, separate cultural groups.
1201	German merchants found the city of Riga.
1290	The Livonian Order completes the forced Christianization of Latvian lands and establishes feudal rule.
1583	The Livonian War results in Latvian territory coming under Polish rule.
1629	Poland loses Latvian territory to Sweden.
1721	Latvia is conquered by czarist Russia.
1850	The Latvian nationalist movement is born. Cultural and political activism increases in the decades that follow.
1914	World War I begins.
1918	Latvia proclaims its independence.
1940	Soviet occupation of Latvia begins.
1941	Latvia is occupied by Nazi troops.
1945	Germany defeated in World War II, Soviets reinstate their occupation of Latvia.
1989	Baltic States unite to peacefully protest communist rule.
1990	Newly elected parliament declares independence will follow a short transition period.
1991	Complete reinstatement of Latvian independence.
2004	Latvia joins NATO and the EU.

FURTHER READING/INTERNET RESOURCES

Dreifelds, Juris. *Latvia in Transition.* Cambridge: Cambridge University Press, 1996.

Nissinen, Marja. *Latvia's Transition to a Market Economy.* New York: St. Martin's Press, 1999.

Plakans, Andrejs. *Historical Dictionary of Latvia.* Lanham, Md.: Rowman and Littlefield Publishers, 1997.

Plakans, Andrejs. *Latvians: A Short History.* Stanford, Calif.: Hoover Press, 1997.

Skultans, Vieda. *Testimony of Lives: Narrative and Memory in Post-Soviet Latvia.* New York: Routledge, 1997.

Travel Information

www.li.lv

www.lonelyplanet.com

History and Geography

www.countryreports.org

www.workmall.com

Culture and Festivals

www.infoplease.com

www.latinst.lv

Economic and Political Information

www.cia.gov/cia/publications/factbook/index.html www.germany-info.org

www.wikipedia.org

EU Information

europa.eu.int/

Publishers note:

The Web sites listed on this page were active at the time of publication. The publisher is not responsible for Web sites that have changed their addresses or discontinued operation since the date of publication. The publisher will review and update the Web-site list upon each reprint.

FOR MORE INFORMATION

Embassy of Latvia
4325 17th St., NW,
Washington DC 20011
Tel.: 202-726-8213
Fax: 202-726-6785

Latvian Tourist Information Bureau
Skunu 22
Riga, LV 1050, Latvia
Tel.: 7-223-113 - 7 221 731
Fax: 371-7-227-680

U.S. Embassy in Latvia
7 Raina Blvd.
Riga LV-1510, Latvia

European Union
Delegation of the European Commission to the United States
2300 M Street, NW
Washington, DC 20037
Tel.: 202-862-9500
Fax: 202-429-1766

GLOSSARY

accession: The formal acceptance by a state of an international treaty or convention.

agrarian: Relating to farming or rural life.

assimilate: To integrate someone into a larger group in such a way that differences are minimized or eliminated.

autonomous: Self-governing.

autonomy: Political independence and self-government.

biomass: Plant and animal material used as a fuel source.

blocs: Groups of countries with shared aims.

capital: Wealth in the form of money or property.

capitalist: Practicing or supporting capitalism, an economic system based on the private ownership of the means of production and distribution of goods, and characterized by a free market and profit.

compulsory: Required.

coniferous: Used to describe trees with thin, needlelike leaves that produce cones.

demographic: Relating to the study of human populations.

entrepreneurial: Relating to the taking on of risk and benefits of running a business.

excise: A government-imposed tax on domestic goods.

feudal: Relating to feudalism, the legal and social system that existed in medieval Europe.

geothermal: Using the heat of the earth's interior to produce energy.

gross domestic product (GDP): The total market value of all the goods and services produced by a nation during a specified period.

gulags: Prisons or labor camps in the former Soviet Union.

information technology: The use of technologies such as computing and telecommunications to process and distribute information in digital and other forms.

infrastructure: A country's large-scale public systems, services, and facilities that are necessary for economic activity.

nationalism: A strong sense of pride in or devotion to one's country.

neutral: Not belonging to any side in a conflict.

pagan: Someone who does not follow one of the world's major religions, and whose religion might be looked on with suspicion.

propaganda: Information put out by an organization or government to spread and promote a policy, idea, doctrine, or cause.

proximity: Nearness.

ratified: Officially approved.

referendum: A vote by the whole of an electorate on a specific question or questions put to it by a government.

Russification: To make Russian in character or quality; to give the characteristic of being from Russia.

service sector: The part of the economy that provides services rather than products.

solidarity: The act of standing together, presenting a united front.

sovereignty: Self-government free from outside interference.

stagnancy: A period of inactivity.

sustainable: Using the natural resources without destroying an area's ecological balance.

tariff: Tax levied by governments on goods, usually imports.

understory: A layer of small trees and shrubs below the level of the taller trees in a forest.

INDEX

agriculture 35
ancient Latvia 20–21

climate 15
communist rule 27
the Crusades 21

dating systems 21
Daugavpils 49

economy 31–37
education 42
energy sources 35, 37
European Union (EU) 55–72

food and drink 42

geography 12, 15
German rule 21

independence 25–27

Latvia in the EU 69–72
    accession 70
    areas of concern 73
    benefits of membership 70–73
    differing views 70
    the future 73
Liepaja 50

music 45

Polish rule 22

religion 40
Riga 49
rivers and lakes 12–13, 15
Russian rule 22–24

sports 42–43

Swedish rule 22–24

trees, plants, wildlife 15,17

Valmiera 53
Ventspils 50

World War I 24–25
World War II 25, 27

Picture Credits

All photos are by Benjamin Stewart, with the following exceptions:

Used with permission of the European Communities: pp. 54–55, 57, 60, 63, 64

Photos.com: pp. 58, 66

BIOGRAPHIES

AUTHOR

Heather Docalavich first developed an interest in the history and cultures of Eastern Europe through her work as a genealogy researcher. She currently resides in Hilton Head, South Carolina, with her four children.

SERIES CONSULTANT

Ambassador John Bruton served as Irish Prime Minister from 1994 until 1997. As prime minister, he helped turn Ireland's economy into one of the fastest-growing in the world. He was also involved in the Northern Ireland Peace Process, which led to the 1998 Good Friday Agreement. During his tenure as Ireland's prime minister, he also presided over the European Union presidency in 1996 and helped finalize the Stability and Growth Pact, which governs management of the euro. Before being named the European Commission Head of Delegation in the United States, he was a member of the convention that drafted the European Constitution, signed October 29, 2004.

The European Commission Delegation to the United States represents the interests of the European Union as a whole, much as ambassadors represent their countries' interests to the U.S. government. Matters coming under European Commission authority are negotiated between the commission and the U.S. administration.